Copyright © 2010 Ramona Thomas Nickens
All rights reserved.

ISBN: 1453802010
ISBN 13: 9781453802014

To Michael (Bubba) Robinson,

May Kyndle's journey be an inspiration to you. Here's to your health!

Lonna

6/16/12

It's morning. Kyndle's mother looks out her bedroom window to gage the weather. She notes it's another foggy day at Fog City Ranch.

She enters Kyndle's bedroom to wake him singing, "Kyndle time to get up." Normally he quickly stirs, gets up and greets his mother; but this day is different. Kyndle continues sleeping. His mother gently nudges him awake uttering, "Kyndle get up or you'll be late to school."

"I don't feel good." He declares.

Concerned, his mother wants to know "What's the matter?"

"My ears hurt and everything looks fuzzy." Kyndle explains.

"Get dressed. We're going to see Dr. Wizmagic right away." She urges.

Kyndle likes Doctor Wizmagic because she's different from other doctors. She makes potions to cure her patients.

Quickly reaching the doctor's office. They register, sit and wait to be called. Within a twinkle of his eye, Dr. Wizmagic directs them to wait in her office. She announces, "I'll be back in a blink of an eye."

In a flash they both hear knocking at the door. It's the doctor. Nervously Kyndle calls "Come in." Dr. Wizmagic greets him and his mother again. Then asks, "How are you feeling today Kyndle?" "I don't feel good, my ears and eyes hurt." The Dr. checks his eyes. Next she grabs the flashlight. It's an otoscope. She uses it to look inside Kyndle's ears. Musing, "I see why your ears hurt."

In the doctor's office, Kyndle looks at funny shaped bottles. Each bottle has different matter inside.

Kyndle watches Doctor Wizmagic pour the following ingredients into a large bowl:

A drop of yellow gooey liquid.

Next,

a squirt of stinky red fluid.

Finally,

a dollop of a slimy green mush.

She stirs and stirs the mixture. It becomes an awful smelly brown concoction. "It stinks!" Kyndle blurts out.

He didn't want this concoction anywhere near him. "You don't drink it. It goes in your ears." The doctor makes clear. Kyndle feels relief.

"This will rid you of your cooties," the wacky doctor exclaims. "Cooties?!" He shrieks.

"When I was a kid we called them Cooties. Actually they're nasty germs living in the world that sometimes enter our bodies," Dr. Wizmagic explains.

The doctor sucks up the brown goo from the bowl with the rubber ear dropper. She squeezes the goo into Kyndle's ears. It feels like worms crawling inside.

Shuddering and hunching his shoulders, he wonders to himself; what's happening inside my ears?

His ears POP! He's able to hear with a clarity he's never heard.

Next he starts to blink his eyes uncontrollably. Open shut, open shut, open shut. Regaining control of his eyes, he sees with a sharpness he's never seen.

The doctor warns Kyndle's mother. "His sight and hearing will be sharper than others until the potion wears off."

The potion is starting to work. Sounds become much louder to Kyndle.

Almost instantly Kyndle starts feeling better. Thrilled his mother

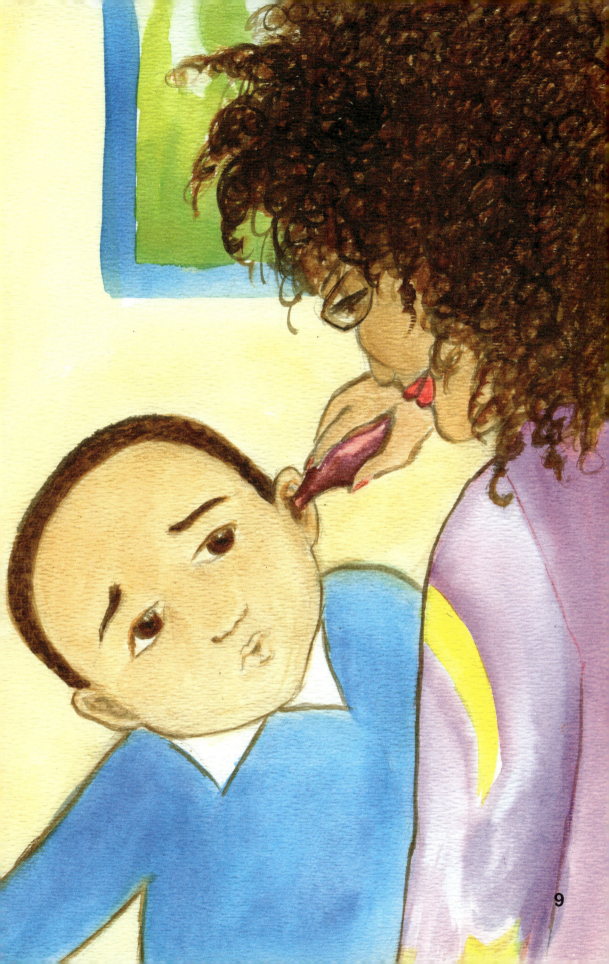

psst, psst, psst, psst, psst, psst, psst

psst

wants to celebrate. She proposes, "Let's make my great grandmother's cookie recipe."

Kyndle loves making cookies with his mother. His excitement can't be contained. He shows it with a huge grin. Which quickly turns into a frown as the shrill his mother's voice pierces his ears. He wonders, Wow! Why is she talking so loud?!

They leave the doctor's office and make a beeline directly to the grocery store. While in route, Kyndle says "Thank you Mom." His mother replies, "You're welcome, I'm glad you're feeling better."

They reach the baking aisle. First on the list is flour. His mother reaches for the bleached flour when suddenly Kyndle hears, "Psst, psst..." He's alarmed. Then he hears it again, "Psst, psst....." The sound is coming from the shelf. "Psst, psst..." "Discovering the sound is coming from the wheat flour, He's shocked!

The wheat flour says in a loud booming voice, "Tell your mama to choose me! I'm better than bleached flour."

Before Kyndle answers, another voice chimes in.

"Little man over here", the bleached flour blurts out. "I'm soft and sweet and very good to eat. Ask your mother to buy me."

Kyndle asks, "What's better mom, wheat flour or bleached flour? His mother grabs both the wheat and bleached flour from the shelf.

"Let's look at the nutrition label." She recommends. "They discover the wheat flour is higher in fiber and has more nutrients."

Next she explains to Kyndle "Nutrients are the good stuff for our bodies. They help us grow strong so we live longer healthier lives."

Placing the bleached flour on the shelf, she puts the wheat flour into the cart. Elated to be selected, the wheat flour give each other high five with floury hands.

Kyndle pushes the cart a bit further down the aisle to the sugar. When his mother reaches for the refined sugar the organic brown sugar yells out, "STOP HER!"

Kyndle yells "STOP!" Annoying his mother with the outburst, she checks his forehead for fever. "Are you sure you're feeling better?" She asks.

Then the organic brown sugar speaks, "Come on, help a Sista out. Tell your mama not to buy the refined sugar."

"I don't know how to stop her." Kyndle pleads.

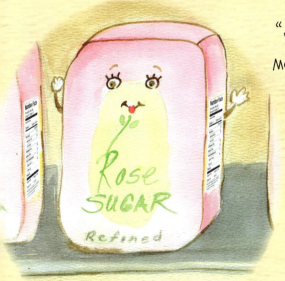

"Just tell your mama that I have more nutrients, you know, more of the good stuff for your body."

Kyndle hears another voice; it's the refined sugar. "Please ask your mother to buy me."

Confused he asks, "Is organic sugar better for us or is refined sugar better?" "Let's check out the nutrition label." His mother advises.

The organic sugar is right. The natural ingredients lessen our chances of getting tooth decay." "We're buying organic sugar." She places it into the shopping cart.

Laughing so hard they burst at the seams, sending brown sparkles into the air. It's like fireworks on the fourth of July. The organic sugars have a real victory celebration.

His temporary power makes him feel really special. He wishes this feeling would last forever. Unfortunately the potion will eventually wear off.

He thinks, *too bad mom can't experience this.*

Reaching the eggs, Kyndle is filled with curiosity. He asks "Are brown eggs better for me? Do they have more good stuff for our bodies?"

His mother didn't answer his question right away. Instead she asks him "If you lay an egg, what color will it be?"

Pondering his mother's question he responds, "I can't lay an egg." Then it hit him. "Brown!"

"You know that's right!" Mom agrees.

She teaches him explaining, "Chickens are sort of like people. Usually white hens lay white eggs and reddish brown hens lay brown eggs. They look different on the outside but have the same nutritional value inside. With the same good stuff for our bodies. Then she gives the carton of brown eggs to Kyndle. All of a sudden he blurts out, "Why did you choose the brown eggs?"

"I'm spending extra money because these eggs remind me of your big beautiful brown eyes." Her compliment makes him blush and smile.

Kyndle hears singing. The eggs are singing a Hallelujah song.

"Speaking on behalf of my fellow eggs, please thank your mama for us." The soprano egg says to Kyndle. "We rarely get chosen because we seldom go on sale."

Kyndle's stomach growls. He feels hungry. "Are we almost done?" He asks.

His mother answers, "Yes, but we need to get the spices. So they round up the cloves, ground ginger and cinnamon.

Noticing how many foods are naturally brown Kyndle shares his idea, "Let's name great grandmama's cookies "Grandma's Brown Cookies made with the good stuff."

"Cool, I like that!"

"Oh my goodness! I forgot to get the rice. Sweetie, get a bag of rice and hurry." Mom pleads.

"What kind?" Kyndle groans.

Instructing him she replies, "You choose."

Learning so much about making healthy food choices Kyndle quickly grabs the brown rice.

The white rice asks the brown rice, "Why did he choose you?"

Kyndle listens as the brown rice gives a boastful explanation. "We both started out with lots of nutrients. Unfortunately, most of your nutrients are gone. Like potatoes we have more nutrients when our outer layer of skin stays intact. I still have my whole bran but you don't. You've been refined. You cook fast. You are fluffy and moist too! In fact, I hear you taste really good, but I am so much better for the human body. Don't feel bad, we're still family little sis. We started

out the same, but your brown bran covering was removed. The little man only chose me because I'm simply a healthier choice."

Kyndle takes the brown rice, turns around and is startled by Dr. Wizmagic whose standing behind him. "Are you feeling better?" She asks.

"Yes Doctor, I always feel better with your magical potions."

Dr. Wizmagic chuckles and encourages him, "Continue making healthy food choices and you won't need to see me for a long time."

His mother is waiting in line when they join her. Dr. Wizmagic notices all the healthy foods in their cart.

She says to his mother, "I see you've made healthy selections. Keep up the good work and Kyndle will continue to grow healthy and strong."

"Thanks Dr. Wizmagic," they say in unison.

Mom pays for the groceries and they go home.

Kyndle is thankful Dr. Wizmagic made his experience magical, educational and fun!

With his mother's help, he mixes all of the ingredients together to make Grandma's Brown Cookies made with the good stuff.

Beautiful brown cookies are removed from the oven. Kyndle can hardly wait to sink his teeth into them. He hopes his dad comes home soon. He wants him to taste the cookies while they're hot.

He takes a bite. Vamoose his special power vanishes. His hearing and sight return to normal. He's officially cootie free!

Grandma's Brown Cookie Recipe

In a mixing bowl Kyndle added the following ingredients:

1/2c butter
1/2c brown sugar
1 large egg
1/2c organic pumpkin
1/2c raw turbinado sugar
¼ c molasses unsulphured
¼ tsp salt
½ tsp vanilla
2c organic whole grain spelt flour
1 ½ tsp ground cinnamon
½ tsp ground cloves
2 tsp ground ginger
½ tsp baking soda

Preheat oven 375 degrees
Beat butter, molasses, pumpkin and brown sugar
Next add egg, vanilla and continue beating
Now add dry ingredients, flour, cinnamon, cloves, ginger, baking soda and salt continue mixing
Chill dough for 30 minutes.
After dough chills, remove from refrigerator.
Make 1 inch balls by rolling dough in your hands
Place parchment paper on cookie sheets and put balls approximately 2 inches apart then flatten slightly with the base of a drinking glass.
Bake for 12-15 minutes
Let cool for 5 minutes, sink your teeth in and enjoy the magic!

Optional: carob chips, nuts, granola, oats, raisins, cranberries, or almonds.

Glossary

Potion- Prescription

Musing- Thinks about

Matter- Stuff

Concoction- Mixture

Shrieks- High pitched scream

Appeal- Request for help

Pondering- Thinking over

Plead- Request

Startled- Surprised

Acknowledges- to admit to be real or true

Shuddering- Shaking

To boot- in addition; besides

Germ- bacteria or virus

Shrill- high-pitched and piercing in sound

Nutrients- source of nourishment

Elated- very happy

Refine- to make fine

Bleach- remove color from

Intact- not changed, undamaged

Organic- natural

Unison- together

Bran- the outer layer of cereal grain

Curiosity- desire to learn or know

Beeline- a direct route traveled quickly

Goo- a thick or sticky substance

Register- a book which records of events and names are kept.

Dedication

Be encouraged to have acceptance of all that is natural in you and the world.

Acknowledgement

I owe the success of my first book "Grandma's Brown Cookies" to friends, relatives, teachers, librarians, independent book store owners and school administrators throughout the San Francisco Bay Area. Thank you so much. Your support encourages me to continue to write stories to educate the human race. I look forward to spreading the word about the beauty of all natural organic brown ingredients with this story.

To my illustrator Tammy Artis, I look forward to our work on future projects. To my editor, Yvetta D. Franklin, I'm so thankful for the connection we've made. Your advice will remain with me forever. To my champion, Deborah Day; thank you for promoting my book with fervor. I hope you'll continue. To my aunt Mary, I am truly amazed by your support and enthusiasm. Thank you for sharing my story with all of your friends.

To my loving husband, children, parents, and siblings thanks for caring and always being there for me. I love you all.

Made in the USA
Charleston, SC
26 April 2012